No portion of this book may be reproduced in whole or in part, whatsoever, except for passages excerpted for the pu prior written permission of the publisher. For informat copies, please contact: TitleTown Publishing, LLC P.O. 54307-12093 920.737.8051 | titletownpub

Publisher: Tracy C. Ertl
Publisher's Cataloging-in-Publication
(Provided by Cassidy Cataloguing Services, Inc.).
ISBN: 9781955047432

Names: Lloyd, Lisa (Lisa K.), author. | Lopez Nunez, Mariana, illustrator.
Title: Fun at the beach / Lisa Lloyd ; illustrations by Mariana Lopez Nunez.
Description: Green Bay, WI : TitleTown Publishing, [2024] | Series: Adventures with Miles. | Audience: Children. | Summary: Miles sees the mail truck down the street and watches in anticipation as it pulls in front of his house. He squeals delightfully and asks his dad to help him get the mail. He notices YaYa has drawn a turtle, a sandcastle, and a bunch of seashells on the outside. Miles opens the box and is met with the sweet face of a stuffed sea turtle. As he digs deeper into the box, he finds a pail and shovel. He knows YaYa sends him three things in each surprise box, so he knows one more surprise is waiting for him. At the bottom of the box is a delicate bag of beautiful sea shells. He looks at the turtle, pail, and shells and knows precisely the adventure they are taking together. YaYa and Miles are headed to the beach! He can hardly wait to run through the water, build a sandcastle and hunt for the perfect shell. Miles knows the adventure has just begun. He can't wait to spend the day at the beach with his YaYa!--Publisher.

Identifiers: ISBN: 9781955047432 (trade paperback)
Subjects: LCSH: Grandmothers--Juvenile fiction. | Beachgoers--Juvenile fiction. | Beaches—Juvenile fiction. | Seashore--Juvenile fiction. | Sea turtles--Juvenile fiction. | Sandcastles—Juvenile fiction. | Shells--Juvenile fiction. | Adventure and adventurers--Juvenile fiction. | CYAC:Grandmothers--Fiction. | Beaches--Fiction. | Seashore--Fiction. | Sea turtles--Fiction. | Sandcastles--Fiction. | Shells--Fiction. | Adventure and adventurers--Fiction. | LCGFT: Action and adventure fiction. | BISAC: JUVENILE FICTION / Family / Multigenerational. | JUVENILE FICTION / Action & Adventure / General.Classification: LCC: PZ7.1.L589 F86 2024 | DDC: [E]--dc23

Adventures With Miles
FUN AT THE BEACH

Lisa Lloyd

Illustrations by Mariana López Nuñez

TITLETOWN
PUBLISHING

Fun at the Beach Adventures with Miles
Copyright (C) 2024 Lisa Lloyd. All Rights Reserved.

for miles
love yaya

Today is an exciting day for *Miles!*
His grandmother, whom he calls *yaya,*
sent him a surprise box for their next adventure.

He peers out of the front window of his house,
waiting for the *mail* to arrive.
Miles and YaYa live far from each other
and don't see one another often,
but that doesn't stop them from
having adventures together.

Miles sees the *mail truck* down the street and watches in anticipation as it pulls in front of his house.

He jumps up and down
and asks his Dad to help him get the mail.
Miles carries the box across the yard
and climbs the porch steps back into the house.

He sits on the living room floor and looks at the *box*.
He notices YaYa has drawn a turtle,
a sandcastle, and a bunch of seashells on the outside.

Miles opens the box and is met with the sweet face of a *sea turtle*. As he digs deeper into the box, he finds a *blue bucket* and a *red shovel*.

He knows YaYa sends him three things in each surprise box,
so he knows one more surprise is waiting for him.
At the bottom of the box is a bag of beautiful *seashells*.
He looks at the turtle, bucket, and shells and knows they are
heading to the beach!

After a short drive, Miles and YaYa arrive at the *beach*. The smell of the salty water and the sound of the waves welcome them as they get out of the car.

YaYa gets the *beach bag* filled with their adventure items and grabs Miles hand to walk to the beach.
He holds YaYa's hand and hugs
the stuffed sea turtle from the surprise box.

As they walk, YaYa explains to Miles that about two months ago, a momma sea turtle made a long *journey* swimming to this special beach, crawled out of the ocean, and searched for the perfect place to lay her eggs. She dug a deep hole and carefully placed the turtle eggs inside.

She covered it with sand to keep them safe and warm and returned to the sea. They have been growing inside their eggs but are now ready to *hatch*. The crowd starts pointing, and YaYa helps Miles to the front so he can see the first baby sea turtle crawl out of the hole.

The turtle is dark green and
about the size of a small pancake.
Miles claps with excitement at the sight of the *tiny turtle*
Within a few minutes, the sand in front of them is dotted
with almost a hundred turtles.

The turtles use their little *flippers* to slide across the sand, heading to the ocean. After most of the turtles have reached the water, the crowd leaves. Miles and YaYa don't move. They stand hand in hand and cheer on the last little turtle until it swims away.

Miles waves goodbye and turns, looking up at his YaYa.
The sun hits his face,
and she can see the *curiosity* in his eyes.

There are more fun things to do on their beach *adventure*, but for now, Miles and YaYa sit together. Their toes are in the *sand* and they talk about the tiny turtles and the adventures awaiting them in the big blue ocean.

Miles and YaYa begin to look for the perfect place to lay out their *beach towels.* YaYa spreads out the towels and puts up the beach umbrella. Miles likes the way the warm sand feels on his feet.

He sees other children using a shovel and a bucket
to dig in the sand and
making something that looks like a *castle*.
He knows what the shovel and bucket
in the surprise box are for!

He places his stuffed turtle in the *beach bag* and pulls out the red shovel and blue bucket. Miles and YaYa begin digging in the sand and filling the bucket.

YaYa shows Miles how to pat it down and quickly turn the bucket over to reveal a perfect shape.
It's *magic* to Miles.
He wants to build the biggest sand castle ever built.

Miles and YaYa work for a while,
creating the most *beautiful castle* on the beach.
The sun is hot, and they are getting hungry.
Being a sand castle builder is hard work!

They sit on their beach towels under the *umbrella* and enjoy the lunch YaYa packed for them. The day has gone by fast, and it will be time to head home soon, but Miles knows their day at the beach is not over yet.

While YaYa packs up,
she tells Miles she has one more surprise.
He wonders if it has anything to do with the *bag of shells*
in the surprise box.

YaYa takes Miles's hand, and they head closer to the water. She shows him the *seashells* the waves have brought onto the sand. He can't believe his eyes. There are shells everywhere! Big ones and small ones, in many different shapes and colors.

He starts picking up as many shells
as his little hands can hold and then has an idea.
He pulls out the blue bucket from the beach bag
and uses it to hold his *treasures.*
YaYa and Miles fill the bucket together
and then sit down on the beach to
watch the *waves* crash onto the sand.

They talk about the turtles, the biggest sand castle ever built, and the blue bucket *overflowing* with shells.

Miles and YaYa begin the walk back to the car. Their day at the beach is over, but Miles can't wait for the next surprise box to arrive to find out what adventure his YaYa has planned for them *next.*